A NEW HOME

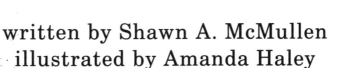

written by Shawn A. McMullen
illustrated by Amanda Haley

CIP DATA AVAILABLE
Library of Congress Catalog Card Number 91-43071
The Standard Publishing Company, Cincinnati, Ohio.
A division of Standex International Corporation.
© 1992 by The Standard Publishing Company. All rights reserved.

Printed in the United States of America   24-03866

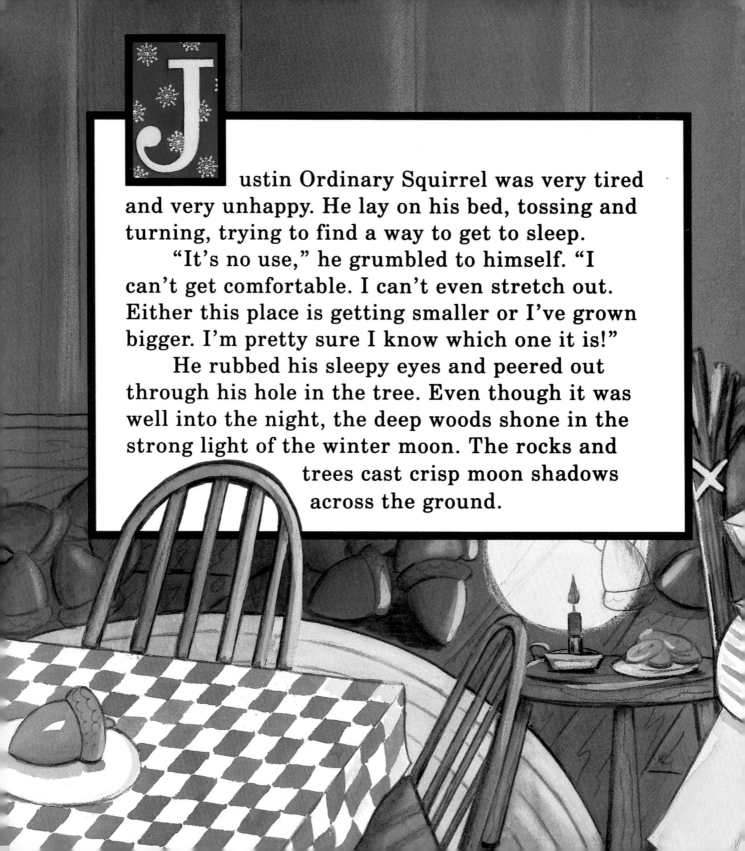

Justin Ordinary Squirrel was very tired and very unhappy. He lay on his bed, tossing and turning, trying to find a way to get to sleep.

"It's no use," he grumbled to himself. "I can't get comfortable. I can't even stretch out. Either this place is getting smaller or I've grown bigger. I'm pretty sure I know which one it is!"

He rubbed his sleepy eyes and peered out through his hole in the tree. Even though it was well into the night, the deep woods shone in the strong light of the winter moon. The rocks and trees cast crisp moon shadows across the ground.

"Of all the times to outgrow a house," Justin complained, "I have to pick winter. I should be eating and napping instead of tossing and turning. I've got to find a new home—and soon!"

He looked out over the vast deep woods. "There just has to be a big, comfortable home waiting for me out there somewhere, and I intend to find it!"

And with that Justin laid his weary head on his paws and tried once more to drift into that much-needed sleep.

With the morning sun peeking through cloud-filled skies, Justin, who never did quite get to sleep, rose to his feet with a yawn and half a stretch. He would have stretched out fully, only there wasn't enough room. He glanced outside and then at the tiny pile of acorns in a corner.

"I'd better gather some more of those," he said to himself. "It looks like we might be in for a storm." He sighed. "I guess house hunting will just have to wait."

Justin braced himself against the winter wind as he scurried down the trunk of his tree and out into the deep woods. He knew exactly where he was going. He had buried several acorns at the foot of a fallen tree in a far corner of the woods.

By the time Justin reached the fallen tree and began digging in the frozen ground, the morning sky had grown darker and a light snow began falling. He was so busy with his digging that he paid no attention when the wind grew stronger and the snow started piling up around him. By the time he did notice the storm, the deep woods was already blanketed with snow and ice and a bitter wind was cutting through his fur. Justin shivered.

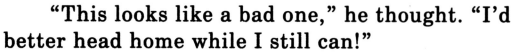

"This looks like a bad one," he thought. "I'd better head home while I still can!"

A small branch, holding a cluster of acorns, lay at his feet. Justin clenched it between his teeth and hurriedly set off through the blinding storm.

Justin soon realized the storm was worse than he thought. The snow was already so deep he had to jump at every step. It stuck to his fur and weighed him down. Ice froze to his face and eyelids. He stopped for a moment to shake it off but was almost buried by the drifting snow. The fierce wind howled around him as it slipped through the tall trees, causing branches to creak and moan and crack. "I'll never make it back home," Justin thought fearfully. "I'll have to find someplace to wait out the storm."

Justin began climbing one tree after another, desperately looking for a place to escape the storm. The acorns he carried and the ice on the tree trunks made his search difficult and dangerous. But for all his searching, he found nothing. The weary, frozen Justin finally sank into the snow. "I give up," he moaned. "I can't go on. There's no place to hide."

Just then Justin caught sight of something that gave him hope. Off in the distance he could barely make out an opening half way up a large oak tree. Summoning his last ounce of strength, Justin trudged through the heavy snow and slowly made his way up the icy trunk. Cold, wet, and exhausted, Justin climbed into the hole, curled up on its floor and fell fast asleep.

He awoke much later to discover that the storm had passed. The dark clouds had disappeared. A blanket of pure, white snow enveloped the deep woods and the ice-covered trees sparkled like giant, odd-shaped diamonds in the afternoon sun. Here and there great branches had fallen to the ground, unable to support the weight of snow and ice. Justin breathed in the beautiful scene. He was glad to be alive. Glad to have survived the storm. Glad to have found this hole in the tree.

"This hole!" Justin said with surprise. For the first time since he had crawled into the hole to escape the storm, Justin realized where he was. He looked around, hardly able to believe his eyes. He was standing in the middle of a large, abandoned den. Without hesitation he exclaimed, "This is it! It's perfect! This will be my new home!"

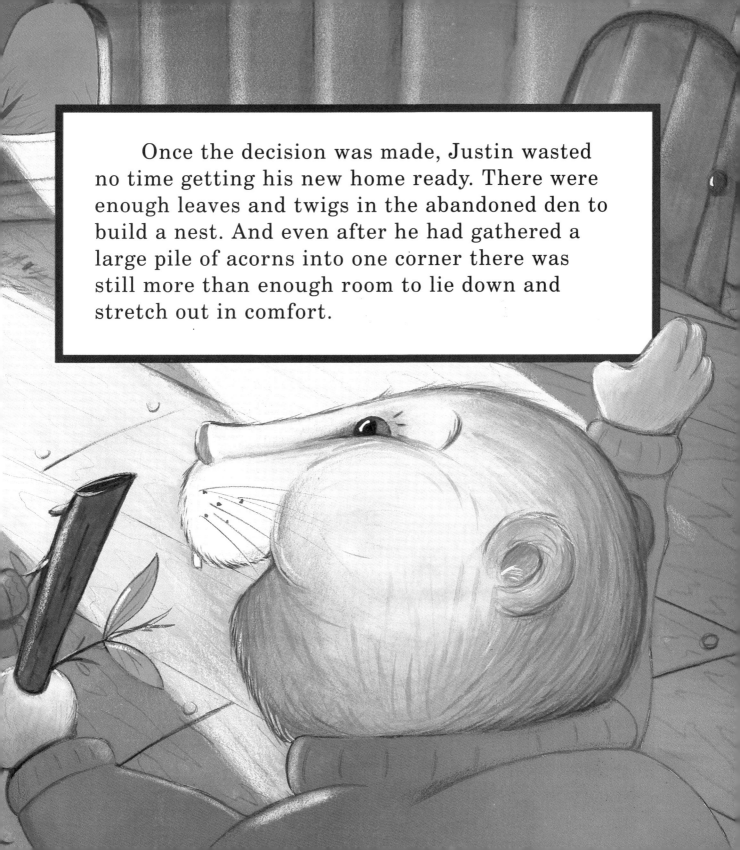

Once the decision was made, Justin wasted no time getting his new home ready. There were enough leaves and twigs in the abandoned den to build a nest. And even after he had gathered a large pile of acorns into one corner there was still more than enough room to lie down and stretch out in comfort.

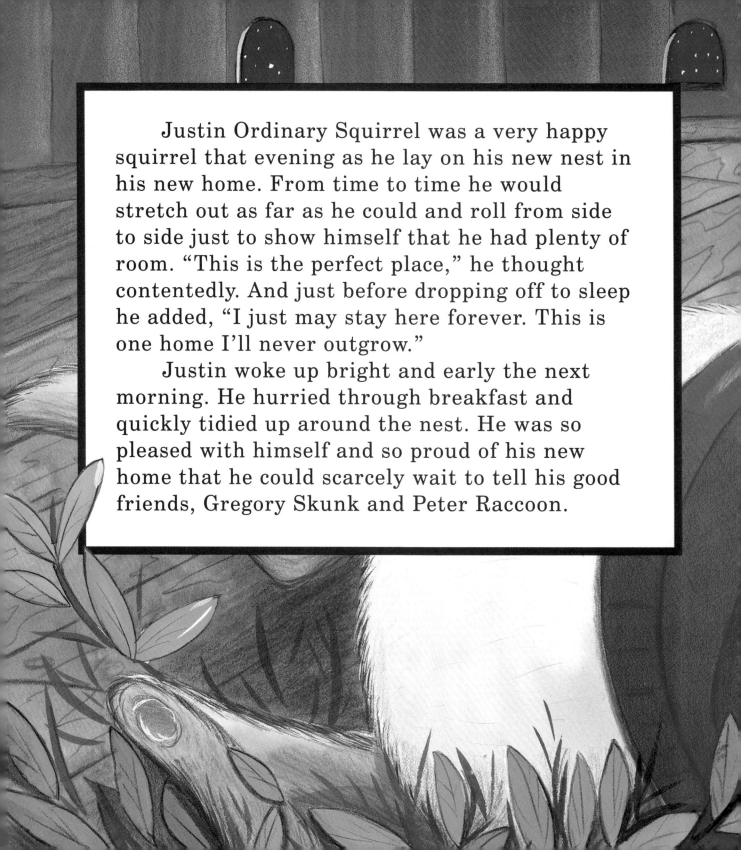

Justin Ordinary Squirrel was a very happy squirrel that evening as he lay on his new nest in his new home. From time to time he would stretch out as far as he could and roll from side to side just to show himself that he had plenty of room. "This is the perfect place," he thought contentedly. And just before dropping off to sleep he added, "I just may stay here forever. This is one home I'll never outgrow."

Justin woke up bright and early the next morning. He hurried through breakfast and quickly tidied up around the nest. He was so pleased with himself and so proud of his new home that he could scarcely wait to tell his good friends, Gregory Skunk and Peter Raccoon.

Justin scurried down his tree and bounced across the snow-covered floor of the deep woods to Gregory's home. He came to the entrance and peered down into the hollow room Gregory had dug beneath the roots of a large evergreen. Gregory wasn't there. "Maybe he's with Peter," Justin concluded.

And he hurried off to the giant beech tree where Peter made his home. He arrived just in time to see Peter sliding down the trunk to join the waiting Gregory. "Hey you guys!" Justin called, "I've got some great news. . . ." But before he could finish he was interrupted by Gregory.

"And we've got some bad news," Gregory said sadly. "I just heard it this morning. I came to get Peter, and then we were coming to get you. I thought maybe we could help somehow."

"Help?" Justin asked uncertainly. "Help who? What's wrong?"

"It's Solomon Squirrel and his family," Gregory said solemnly. "They lost their home during the ice storm yesterday. A limb above their den broke under the weight of the ice. It split their tree in half and destroyed their home. Now here they are in the middle of winter with no place to live."

"Come on, Justin," Peter urged. "Let's go see whether we can help." Justin immediately fell in step with his friends, forgetting all about what he came to tell them.

As they approached the tree where the squirrel family had lived, they noticed that several other animals had also come to offer help. Everyone meant well, but no one seemed to know what to say or do. Solomon's wife, Anna, hugged her three youngsters, encouraging them not to cry. "Don't worry, dears," she said reassuringly, "we'll find a new home."

"I'd like to know where," said a discouraged Solomon in response. "It's the middle of winter. Dens big enough for a family of five aren't easy to come by." Anna held her little ones more tightly.

Everyone remained speechless. The home was hopelessly destroyed and no one could think of even a single place in the deep woods that wasn't already occupied.

Suddenly Justin spoke up. "I've got an idea." Everyone turned and looked at him. "You can have my old place. I just moved out yesterday. It's not very big, but it could hold you through the winter. . . ."

Justin's voice trailed off into silence. He paused, stared at the ground, then lifted his head with an embarrassed grin. "No," he corrected, "you can't have my old place." Everyone was shocked. Justin continued. "You can have my new place!" he said with enthusiasm. "It's much bigger and it comes with a brand-new nest and a fresh supply of acorns. It's ready to move into right now."

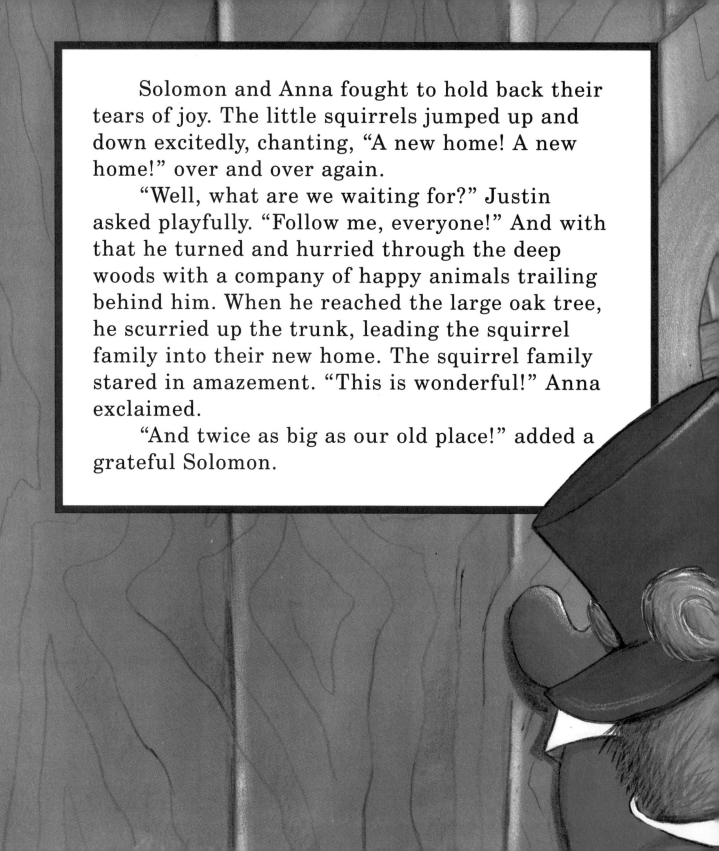

Solomon and Anna fought to hold back their tears of joy. The little squirrels jumped up and down excitedly, chanting, "A new home! A new home!" over and over again.

"Well, what are we waiting for?" Justin asked playfully. "Follow me, everyone!" And with that he turned and hurried through the deep woods with a company of happy animals trailing behind him. When he reached the large oak tree, he scurried up the trunk, leading the squirrel family into their new home. The squirrel family stared in amazement. "This is wonderful!" Anna exclaimed.

"And twice as big as our old place!" added a grateful Solomon.

The little squirrels laughed and cheered as they rolled in the huge nest. Solomon shook Justin's paw. Anna gave him a big hug and kissed him on his furry cheek. Justin blushed. "How can we ever thank you, Justin?" they asked.

"There's no need for that," Justin responded. "I'm just happy you've got a new home."

As the squirrel family began settling into their new home, the other animals quietly slipped away into the deep woods. Peter and Gregory walked with Justin back to his old tree. "Can we help you move back in, Justin?" they asked.

"No thanks," Justin answered. "Everything should be just as I left it." They said good-bye and Justin scampered up the familiar trunk and climbed into the familiar hole.

When evening came, Justin lay on his bed and looked out into the night sky. He felt warm and happy inside, knowing that the squirrel family was safe and snug in their new home. He thought for a moment of how he missed that big open room, but then he curled up in his cramped little nest in his cramped little hole and enjoyed one of the best night's sleep he had ever had.

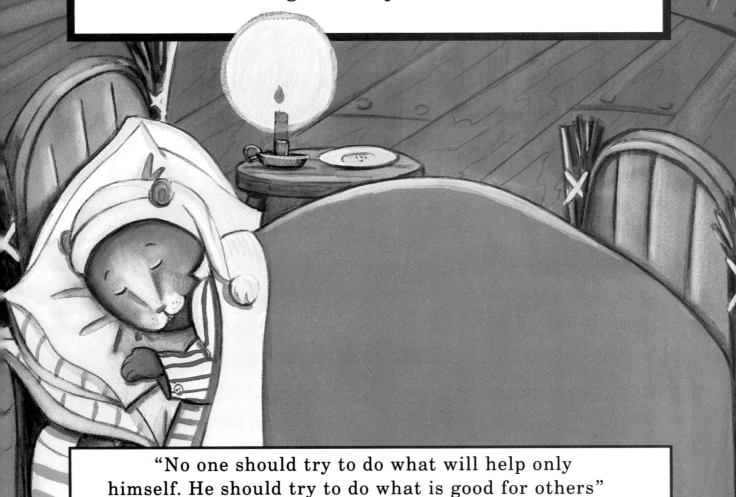

"No one should try to do what will help only himself. He should try to do what is good for others" (1 Corinthians 10:24, ICB).